WOOLFRED CANNOT EAT DANDELIONS

For Robin, who cares about friendship and art—and not so much
about what he can eat. —*CC*

Published by
MAGINATION PRESS
An Educational Publishing Foundation Book
American Psychological Association
750 First Street, NE
Washington, DC 20002

For more information about our books, including a complete catalog, please write to us,
call 1-800-374-2721, or visit our website at www.apa.org/pubs/magination.

Book design by Sandra Kimbell

Printed by Lake Book Manufacturing, Inc., Melrose Park, IL

Library of Congress Cataloging-in-Publication Data
Crangle, Claudine, author, illustrator.
Woolfred cannot eat dandelions : a tale of being true to your tummy / by Claudine Crangle.
pages cm
"American Psychological Association."
Summary: "A young sheep comes to terms with the fact that he can't eat
dandelions without getting sick. Addresses the emotional issues related to
food intolerances"— Provided by publisher.
ISBN 978-1-4338-1672-7 (hardcover) — ISBN 1-4338-1672-5 (hardcover) —
ISBN 978-1-4338-1673-4 (pbk.) — ISBN 1-4338-1673-3 (pbk.) [1. Food intolerance—Fiction.
2. Sheep—Fiction.] I. Title.
PZ7.C85253Wo 2014
[E]—dc23
2013048306

Manufactured in the United States of America
First printing May 2014
10 9 8 7 6 5 4 3 2 1

WOOLFRED CANNOT EAT DANDELIONS

A Tale of Being True to Your Tummy

by Claudine Crangle

Magination Press • Washington, DC
American Psychological Association

Most sheep will eat almost anything they come across…
whether it's good for them or not.

Woolfred, however, was born with a delicate system. Woolfred could not eat dandelions. He had to graze very carefully in the fields around his farm.

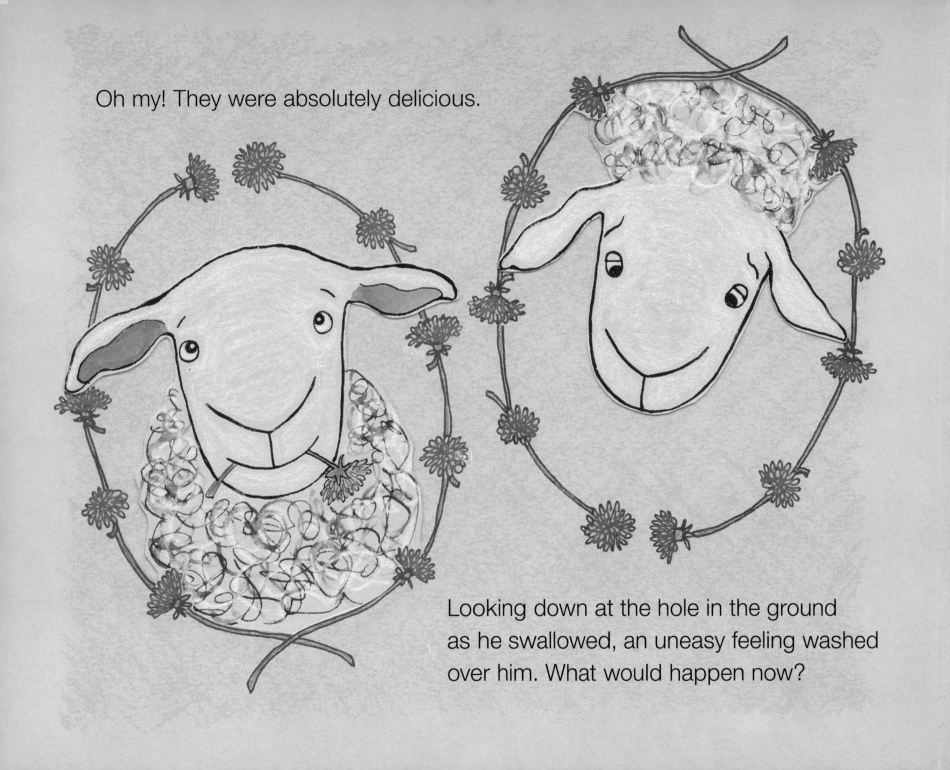

Oh my! They were absolutely delicious.

Looking down at the hole in the ground as he swallowed, an uneasy feeling washed over him. What would happen now?

He didn't have to wait very long to find out.

Gwaaaaglewaaaglewush.

The rest of his flock stopped in their tracks.
What was that funny noise?

Woolfred felt awfully strange. His mouth went dry.
His belly was growing big like a balloon. His legs went all wobbly.

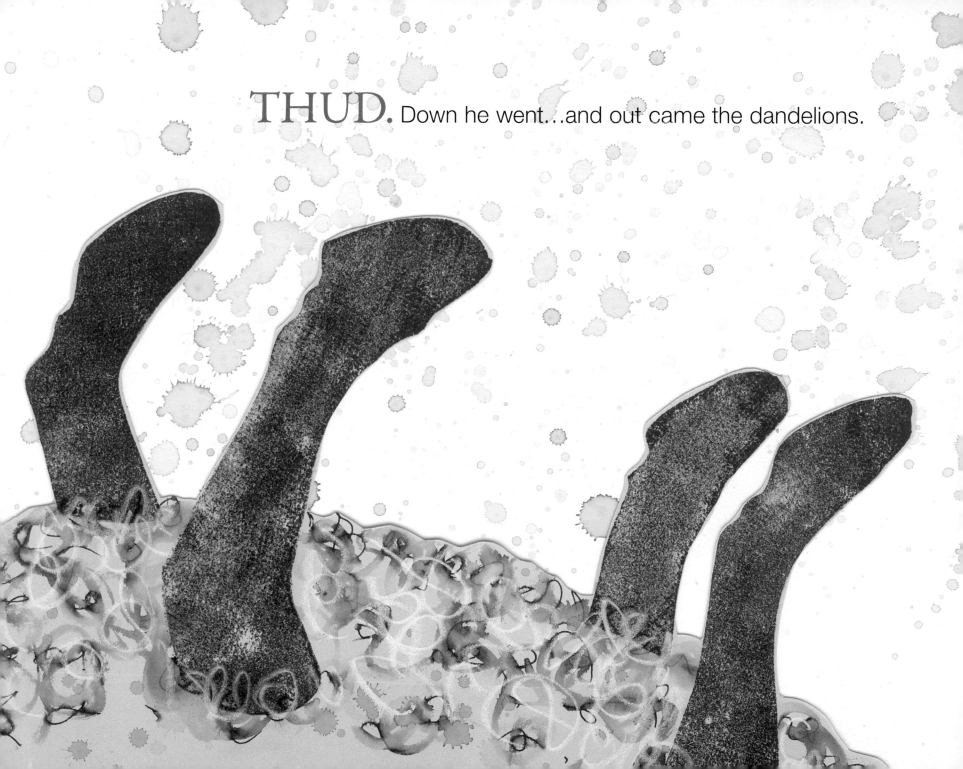

THUD. Down he went…and out came the dandelions.

Woolfred and his dandelions had caused a scene, but it didn't take long for the rest of the flock to go back to normal.

For Woolfred, however, something had changed. He knew what would happen if he ate them, but all Woolfred could think about was dandelions, dandelions, dandelions!

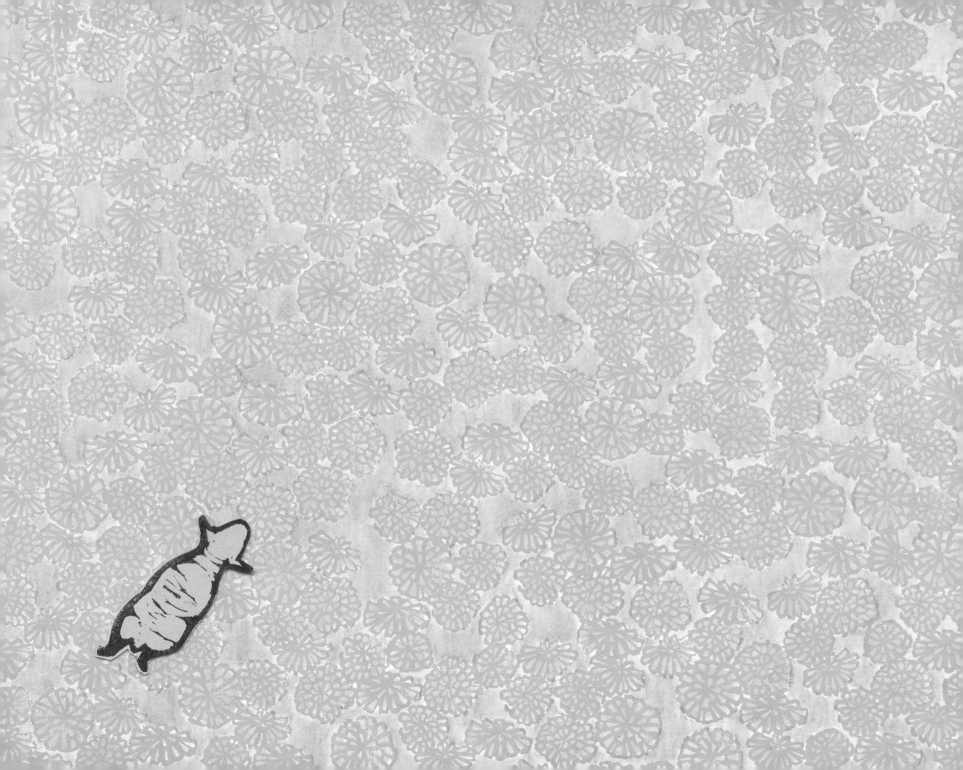

After days of staring at those sunny yellow flowers, he had an idea.
What if he only ate PART of the dandelions?

Carefully avoiding the green parts, he plucked the yellow head from each dandelion stem and chewed with delight.

Mmm…delicious! Woolfred was so happy with his new solution…

The flock begged him to leave the dandelions alone and come play.
But Woolfred had to see what happened when he only ate the green parts.

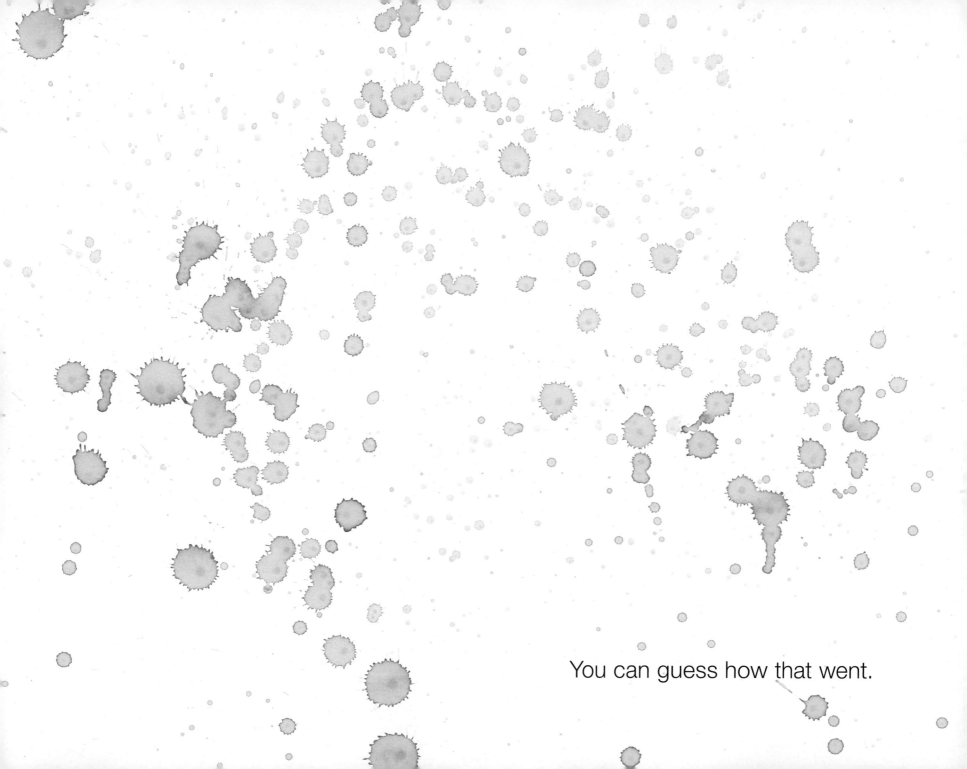

You can guess how that went.

Weeks of eating dandelion parts had left Woolfred weak
and tired. This time, when he hit the ground, he didn't
get up. He lay there for a very long time in a restless sleep.

He didn't like missing jokes, and he certainly enjoyed leaping over puddles. He gave himself a shake. What was he doing just standing there? He was going to miss the fence jumping!

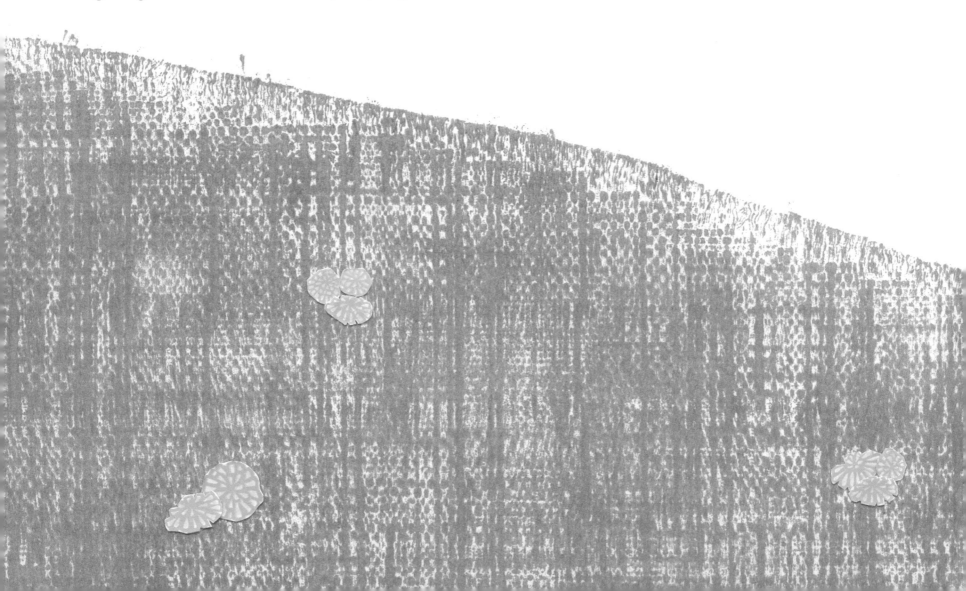

As he charged down the hill to join the others, Woolfred hardly noticed the dandelions, just like he hardly noticed so many things…

Lana sneezes when she's near clover.

Dank rolls in bad smells.

Franklin secretly snacks on flies.

Daisy has no sense of direction.

Marino is terrified of bees.

Lois has ticklish hooves.

Bert likes to scratch his bottom on the ground.

Hoof stutters when he's scared.

Ruby baahs in her sleep.

Woolfred cannot eat dandelions.

NOTE TO PARENTS AND CAREGIVERS
by Frank J. Sileo, PhD

While food intolerances are quite common, children with food intolerances may face challenges that cause them to feel different and deprived. Food and eating are integral parts of our culture, and play a large role in your child's social life. For children with food intolerances, it may be difficult to cope with eating at school, birthday parties, or restaurants. As a parent or caregiver, you can help your child understand her condition and assist her in making good choices when it comes to eating. In addition to these physical and nutritional concerns, however, your child may also need help dealing with the feelings that arise from having a food intolerance.

HOW TO USE THIS BOOK

This is a book that should be read with your child after you have received a proper diagnosis from your doctor. Seeking the advice of a nutritionist may also aid in making appropriate food choices to avoid physical symptoms. Food intolerances are not diseases, nor should they be confused with food allergies. Food allergies can cause reactions that can be severe and life threatening. Food intolerances—such as intolerance to dairy, gluten, eggs, fructose, or yeast, to name a few—are not life threatening, but they can cause uncomfortable symptoms.

When children are diagnosed with a food intolerance, they may experience a range of emotions such as:

- Fear
- Sadness
- Anger
- Loneliness
- Feeling different
- Feeling deprived
- Anxiety
- Depression

Woolfred experiences many of these emotions in the story. As a result, he engages in self-sabotaging behavior—for example, telling himself that he can eat part of the dandelions—that leads him to have further physical symptoms.

Just as Woolfred doesn't want to feel different from the rest of his flock, no child likes to feel different from other children. Children want to be part of the group and don't want their differences highlighted. When children feel different and isolated, those feelings can develop into sadness and deepen into feelings of depression. If children do not learn how to cope with these feelings, they may find themselves like Woolfred—feeling sad, frustrated, and sick.

COPING WITH FOOD INTOLERANCE

Fortunately, there are some strategies you can use to reduce feelings of anxiety, sadness, deprivation, or difference, and develop your and your child's ability to cope with food intolerance. The following are some guidelines for coping with the feelings your child may be experiencing.

Read up. Gain as much information about your child's food intolerance as possible. Knowledge assists us in feeling less helpless. When we feel less helpless, we empower our children with hope. You can obtain information through your pediatrician, a nutritionist or dietician, or reputable online resources such as the American Dietetic Association.

Listen to your child. Keep the lines of communication open with your child. Listen to him with empathy and understanding. Validate your child's negative feelings. Allow him to express feelings in a safe, open, and accepting environment. Find safe places for him to "blow off steam." Set boundaries around acting-out behaviors such as temper tantrums, name-calling, foul language and, in extreme cases, destruction of property. It's important to deal with feelings in age-appropriate ways. Younger children may have more emotional breakdowns because they do not fully understand their food intolerance.

Talk to your child. Depending on your child's age, talk about food intolerances in a way that she will understand. Coach your child to ask questions before eating a meal. This may be more difficult for younger children because they may not be able to focus on this, or they may feel uncomfortable asking adults questions. Older children may feel inhibited because they do not want to be different from their

peers. Help your child memorize a list of foods that may cause problems. Give her simple questions to ask, such as, "Excuse me, is there dairy in this? I am lactose intolerant." If offered a cupcake, she might say, "No thank you. I have a food intolerance to eggs." Role-play with your child and practice what to say and how to handle difficult circumstances such as birthday parties or eating over at a friend's house. Advise your child to state her food intolerance in a calm, matter-of-fact way. If she presents her food intolerance in this way, other kids will be less likely to make a big deal of it. Practice conversations in real-life settings like restaurants or other places where food is served. Not only does practice help your child feel more comfortable, it also allows her to alter the "script" if necessary. Don't forget to praise your child for her efforts.

Model a positive attitude. Children with food intolerances may feel defective. Help them to view their food intolerance as just a part of who they are. Emphasize your child's strengths and other great qualities (e.g., good in math, kind-hearted, good sport, generous friend). Don't allow the food intolerance to define your child. Focus on his strengths, talents, and skills. Encourage him to participate in any activity and teach him that the food intolerance is only a part of who he is; it does not define him. You may want to find role models in the community, media, or sports who have a food intolerance and find out how they may be coping with it. Teach your child that he is not alone. Be careful not to blame yourself for your child's food intolerance. When parents blame themselves, they experience feelings of guilt, sadness, and anxiety which may cause their children to feel worse. If you are feeling overwhelmed by your feelings, it may be a good idea to talk with a mental health professional.

Involve your child in meal planning. Take her food shopping and expose her to alternatives that she can bring to school, have at a birthday party, and eat at home. For birthday parties, plan ahead and speak with the parent hosting the party to find out what food will be served. If you are bringing an alternative treat (such as lactose-free ice cream or popsicles), bring enough for everyone, so that all the children can enjoy what your child is eating. Teach her to read labels and to take an active part in managing her food intolerance. Realizing there are choices and alternatives out there will decrease your child's feelings of sadness and hopelessness. However, keep in mind how your child's food intolerance may affect other family members. Don't deny your other children their feelings or the right to eat foods that are good for them.

Be on the lookout for bullying. Unfortunately, children with food intolerances may be bullied as a result. If you suspect that your child may be getting bullied—either in person or online—it is important that you address it right away. Talk with your child about bullying. Most children keep bullying incidents to themselves. Teach your child assertiveness and coping skills such as speaking up and talking to adults in school, if needed. You may try role-playing to increase your child's comfort with speaking up. Keep the lines of communication open. Talk with your child about his day. You may casually ask him questions such as, "Who did you eat lunch with today?" Check your child's lunchbox to see if he ate all his food. Children may not eat or throw out food alternatives to avoid being seen as different from others. Talk with school personnel (such as the principal, teachers, guidance department, lunch aides, and the school nurse) about your child's food intolerance. If you suspect bullying, or if your child reports bullying as a result of his food intolerance, speak with school personnel immediately. School nurses or health classes can integrate food intolerances in the health/science curriculum. Learning about the physical and emotional aspects may decrease incidences of bullying in and out of the classroom. Lastly, be mindful of teasing or bullying in your own family from siblings. If this is occurring, put a stop to it immediately. If you child is showing more serious effects of bullying it may be helpful for you to seek professional help for your child.

Encourage healthy friendships. Solid friendships provide a great physical and emotional outlet. Social support is an important coping mechanism.

If your child is exhibiting symptoms of a food intolerance, the first step is consulting with your pediatrician or other medical care professional for an accurate diagnosis and treatment plan. It may also be helpful to consult with a nutritionist or dietician to ensure your child is getting the vitamins and minerals necessary for healthy growth of brain function, bones, and body.

As stated earlier, children with food intolerances may struggle with strong feelings such as anxiety, depression, and loneliness. They may be bullied and struggling with the feeling of being different from their peers. If your child is exhibiting strong emotional and behavioral reactions to her condition, it may be advisable to seek the assistance of a qualified mental health professional. Seeing a mental health professional can be beneficial for not only the child but the parent(s) as well. Talking things over with a professional may greatly reduce stress, anxiety, and depression.

Frank J. Sileo, PhD, is a licensed psychologist with a private practice in Ridgewood, New Jersey. He is also lactose intolerant. He has written four children's books, including *Sally Sore Loser: A Story about Winning and Losing; Toilet Paper Flowers: A Story for Children about Crohn's Disease; Hold the Cheese Please: A Story for Children about Lactose Intolerance;* and *Bug Bites and Campfires: A Story for Kids about Homesickness.* His website is Drfranksileo.com.

ABOUT THE AUTHOR AND ILLUSTRATOR

Claudine Crangle grew up just like Woolfred. She has celiac disease and cannot eat any gluten (better known as things like pizza, cookies, bread, donuts, cupcakes, and pasta). She can eat dandelions, but is not particularly fond of how they taste. To learn more visit *claudinecrangle.com*.

ABOUT MAGINATION PRESS

Magination Press is an imprint of the American Psychological Association, the largest scientific and professional organization representing psychologists in the United States and the largest association of psychologists worldwide.

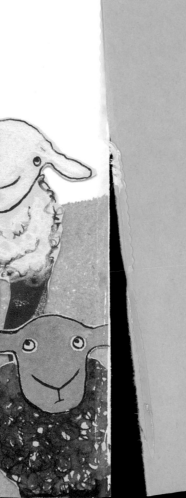

an accurate diagnosis and treatment plan. It may also be helpful to consult with a nutritionist or dietician to ensure your child is getting the vitamins and minerals necessary for healthy growth of brain function, bones, and body.

As stated earlier, children with food intolerances may struggle with strong feelings such as anxiety, depression, and loneliness. They may be bullied and struggling with the feeling of being different from their peers. If your child is exhibiting strong emotional and behavioral reactions to her condition, it may be advisable to seek the assistance of a qualified mental health professional. Seeing a mental health professional can be beneficial for not only the child but the parent(s) as well. Talking things over with a professional may greatly reduce stress, anxiety, and depression.

Frank J. Sileo, PhD, is a licensed psychologist with a private practice in Ridgewood, New Jersey. He is also lactose intolerant. He has written four children's books, including *Sally Sore Loser: A Story about Winning and Losing; Toilet Paper Flowers: A Story for Children about Crohn's Disease; Hold the Cheese Please: A Story for Children about Lactose Intolerance;* and *Bug Bites and Campfires: A Story for Kids about Homesickness.* His website is Drfranksileo.com.

ABOUT THE AUTHOR AND ILLUSTRATOR

Claudine Crangle grew up just like Woolfred. She has celiac disease and cannot eat any gluten (better known as things like pizza, cookies, bread, donuts, cupcakes, and pasta). She can eat dandelions, but is not particularly fond of how they taste. To learn more visit *claudinecrangle.com.*

ABOUT MAGINATION PRESS

Magination Press is an imprint of the American Psychological Association, the largest scientific and professional organization representing psychologists in the United States and the largest association of psychologists worldwide.

peers. Help your child memorize a list of foods that may cause problems. Give her simple questions to ask, such as, "Excuse me, is there dairy in this? I am lactose intolerant." If offered a cupcake, she might say, "No thank you. I have a food intolerance to eggs." Role-play with your child and practice what to say and how to handle difficult circumstances such as birthday parties or eating over at a friend's house. Advise your child to state her food intolerance in a calm, matter-of-fact way. If she presents her food intolerance in this way, other kids will be less likely to make a big deal of it. Practice conversations in real-life settings like restaurants or other places where food is served. Not only does practice help your child feel more comfortable, it also allows her to alter the "script" if necessary. Don't forget to praise your child for her efforts.

Model a positive attitude. Children with food intolerances may feel defective. Help them to view their food intolerance as just a part of who they are. Emphasize your child's strengths and other great qualities (e.g., good in math, kind-hearted, good sport, generous friend). Don't allow the food intolerance to define your child. Focus on his strengths, talents, and skills. Encourage him to participate in any activity and teach him that the food intolerance is only a part of who he is; it does not define him. You may want to find role models in the community, media, or sports who have a food intolerance and find out how they may be coping with it. Teach your child that he is not alone. Be careful not to blame yourself for your child's food

intolerance. When parents blame themselves, they experience feelings of guilt, sadness, and anxiety which may cause their children to feel worse. If you are feeling overwhelmed by your feelings, it may be a good idea to talk with a mental health professional.

Involve your child in meal planning. Take her food shopping and expose her to alternatives that she can bring to school, have at a birthday party, and eat at home. For birthday parties, plan ahead and speak with the parent hosting the party to find out what food will be served. If you are bringing an alternative treat (such as lactose-free ice cream or popsicles), bring enough for everyone, so that all the children can enjoy what your child is eating. Teach her to read labels and to take an active part in managing her food intolerance. Realizing there are choices and alternatives out there will decrease your child's feelings of sadness and hopelessness. However, keep in mind how your child's food intolerance may affect other family members. Don't deny your other children their feelings or the right to eat foods that are good for them.

Be on the lookout for bullying. Unfortunately, children with food intolerances may be bullied as a result. If you suspect that your child may be getting bullied—either in person or online—it is important that you address it right away. Talk with your child about bullying. Most children keep bullying incidents to themselves. Teach your child assertiveness and coping skills such as speaking up

and talking to adults in school, if needed. You may try role-playing to increase your child's comfort with speaking up. Keep the lines of communication open. Talk with your child about his day. You may casually ask him questions such as, "Who did you eat lunch with today?" Check your child's lunchbox to see if he ate all his food. Children may not eat or throw out food alternatives to avoid being seen as different from others. Talk with school personnel (such as the principal, teachers, guidance department, lunch aides, and the school nurse) about your child's food intolerance. If you suspect bullying, or if your child reports bullying as a result of his food intolerance, speak with school personnel immediately. School nurses or health classes can integrate food intolerances in the health/science curriculum. Learning about the physical and emotional aspects may decrease incidences of bullying in and out of the classroom. Lastly, be mindful of teasing or bullying in your own family from siblings. If this is occurring, put a stop to it immediately. If you child is showing more serious effects of bullying it may be helpful for you to seek professional help for your child.

Encourage healthy friendships. Solid friendships provide a great physical and emotional outlet. Social support is an important coping mechanism.

If your child is exhibiting symptoms of a food intolerance, the first step is consulting with your pediatrician or other medical care professional for